A King Production presents…

A Family's Farewell…

A Novella

JOY DEJA KING

Cover concept by Joy Deja King

Graphic design: www.anitaart79.wixsite.com/bookdesign
Typesetting: Anita J.

Library of Congress Cataloging-in-Publication Data;
King, Deja Joy
Stackin' Paper Holiday A Family's Farewell: a novella by Joy Deja King
For complete Library of Congress Copyright info visit;
www.joydejaking.com Twitter: @joydejaking

A King Production
P.O. Box 912, Collierville, TN 38027

A King Production and the above portrayal logo are trademarks of A King Production LLC

This Book is Dedicated To My:

Family, Readers and Supporters.
I LOVE you guys so much. Please believe that!!

Joy Deja King

"Bonds Of Blood And Loyalty Are Both
A Families Greatest Strength And
Deepest Challenge..."

A KING PRODUCTION

Stackin' PAPER

HOLIDAY...

A Family's Farewell

A Novella

JOY DEJA KING

Chapter One

A Somber Christmas Eve

The crystal teardrops of the chandelier sparkled overhead, a stark contrast to the heaviness in Genesis' heart. He stood motionless in the grand foyer, his eyes fixed on the opulent fixture, yet unseeing. The weight of Amir's absence pressed down on him like a physical force.

"My son," Genesis whispered, his voice barely audible. "How am I supposed to do this without you?"

His mind raced, replaying memories of Amir's laugh, smile, his unwavering loyalty to his family, the way he always wanted to do what was right and protect the people he loves. Now, that steadfast presence was gone, leaving a void that threatened to destroy Genesis.

Genesis clenched his fists, struggling to maintain his composure. The evening ahead loomed like a mountain to be climbed, each step fraught with potential pitfalls. He had to be strong, had to present a united front for the family, for the empire he'd built for them but seemed inconsequential now that Amir was longer here.

"I'll make this right, Amir," he vowed silently. "I'll bring Maverick to his knees. I promise. No matter what it takes."

The sound of footsteps echoing through the hallway pulled Genesis from his thoughts. He turned, his breath catching as Talisa appeared, their daughter's small hand clasped in hers.

"Genesis," Talisa said softly, her eyes meeting his. In that moment, a world of understanding passed between them – shared grief, unspoken fears, and a determination to face whatever came next, together.

"Baby girl," Genesis murmured, opening his arms. Talisa stepped into his embrace; their daughter nestled between them. He breathed in the familiar scent of her perfume, drawing strength from her presence.

"How are you holding up?" Talisa asked, her voice muffled against his chest.

Genesis swallowed hard, fighting back the surge of emotion threatening to overwhelm him.

"I'm managing," he replied, his tone carefully controlled. "It's just... we're about to see everyone, and knowing why..."

Talisa pulled back slightly, her hand coming up to cup his face. "We'll get through this," she said firmly, her eyes shining with unshed tears. "For our beautiful son Amir. For our family. That is what he would want."

Genesis nodded, drawing a deep breath. He looked down at their daughter, her innocent face, a reminder of all they had to protect, all they had to lose. "Yeah," he agreed, his resolve strengthening. "We will."

Talisa's fingers intertwined with Genesis', a silent gesture of support that spoke volumes. For a brief moment, Genesis allowed himself to lean into her strength, his shoulders sagging ever so slightly as the weight of their loss pressed down upon him.

"I miss him so much," Genesis whispered, his voice cracking.

Talisa squeezed his hand, her own pain mirrored in her eyes. "I know, baby. I do too."

Their daughter tugged at Genesis' pant leg, her small face upturned and questioning. "Daddy, why are you sad?"

Genesis crouched down, forcing a smile onto his face. "It's complicated, sweetheart. But don't you worry, okay? Daddy's gonna make everything alright."

As he stood, Genesis caught Talisa's eye. No words needed to be spoken. Both knew what needed to be done – it was time to put on their game faces. With a deep breath, Genesis straightened his tie, while Talisa smoothed her dress.

"Ready?" he asked.

Talisa nodded, her chin lifting with determination. "Let's do this," walking out their New York City penthouse.

The driver opened the door for Talisa and Genevieve as they exited the building, followed by Genesis. They made their way to the waiting Bentley, while the tinted SUV pulled up behind them. Their destination: Precious and Supreme's palatial estate for a family's farewell and Christmas celebration.

Precious made her way towards the kitchen, the sounds of bustling activity growing louder with each step. As she pushed through the swinging door, they were engulfed in a whirlwind of sights, sounds, and smells.

The kitchen was a hive of controlled chaos. Chefs in crisp white uniforms moved with practiced precision, their knives flashing as they chopped and diced. The air was thick with the aroma of sizzling meats and fragrant spices, making Precious' mouth water despite the knot in her stomach.

"Smells good in here," she commented, her eyes scanning the room. "Everything on schedule?"

The head chef, a stocky man with a salt-and-pepper beard, looked up from a steaming pot. "Yes. Dinner will be ready right on time."

Precious nodded, her mind already racing ahead to the evening to come. "Good. Make sure everything's perfect. We got a lot riding on tonight."

Amidst the culinary frenzy, Precious stood like an island of calm, her dark eyes surveying every detail with laser focus. As Supreme approached, she turned to him, her face softening with genuine concern.

"Hi, my love," Precious said, her voice sweet and warm. "How are you feeling?"

Supreme managed a weak smile. "Honestly, not good. But one day at a time. I'm still wrapping my mind around the fact that Amir is gone. I can only imagine what Genesis and Talisa are going through."

Precious leaned in and gave Supreme a soft kiss on his cheek. "I know, which is why I want tonight to be special. It won't bring Amir back, but I hope our love and this Christmas celebration can bring some solace to our families and help us begin the healing process of losing Amir."

Supreme felt a lump form in his throat at the mention of Amir's name. "I pray you're right," he said exiting out the kitchen.

As Supreme stepped into the spacious room, he was struck by the stark contrast between the opulent setting and the heaviness in his heart. The long mahogany table gleamed under the soft chandelier light, each place setting a work of art with its fine china and crystal glasses.

He ran his fingers along the polished wood, memories flooding his mind. "Damn, Amir," he whispered to himself. Supreme remembered the many times when Amir, Aaliyah and Justina sat at his table while growing up. Pretending they were big shots at some fancy dinner party, with Amir always letting Aaliyah believe she was leading the way. The thought brought a smile to Supreme's face.

Supreme chuckled softly, the sound echoing in the empty room. His eyes fell on the seat Amir would occupy, now painfully realizing he would never fill it again. The laughter died in his throat, replaced by a familiar ache.

"We're gonna make this right, Amir," he vowed silently.

Chapter Two

Gathering Storm

The doorbell chimed, pulling Supreme from his daze. He straightened his suit jacket and made his way back to the foyer, steeling himself for the evening ahead. Precious joined Supreme as they both stood at the entrance, ready to greet their guests together. It was essential to her that they presented a united front.

As the heavy door swung open, Genesis and Talisa entered, their daughter's hand clasped tightly between them.

"Genesis, Talisa, we're so sorry for your loss,"

Precious said, her voice soft but steady. "Thank you for coming tonight."

Genesis nodded; his jaw set in a firm line. "Thank you for having us, Precious."

"Good to see you both," Supreme said, clasping hands with Genesis. silent acknowledgment passing between the two men. They both knew the gravity of the night ahead.

Talisa gave Precious a faint smile, her eyes glistening as if a tear could fall at any moment. "It means a lot to us to be here with family."

The group moved towards the grand dining hall, where the table was set for a feast fit for royalty. The extravagant display served as a stark reminder of their recent loss, casting an even heavier sense of grief over the room.

As more guests trickled in, a palpable tension filled the air. Hushed conversations and sympathetic glances punctuated the subdued atmosphere. Genesis greeted each arrival with a stoic nod against the tide of condolences.

"Genesis," a familiar voice called out. Genesis turned to see T-Roc striding towards him, his face etched with a mix of grief and determination. "Good to see you, but I hate it's under these circumstances."

"Me too," Genesis replied, as the two men embraced. The men exchanged a knowing look, an unspoken alliance forged in the wake of tragedy.

T-Roc leaned in close, his voice low. "I got your back, brother. Maverick will regret what he has done to our families."

Genesis nodded, a flicker of vengeance igniting in his eyes. "Appreciate that. We'll talk more later."

As Talisa came over to speak to T-Roc, the room suddenly fell silent. Genesis turned to see Justina entering, cradling her young son against her chest. The sight of Amir's widow and child hit him like a physical blow.

Justina's eyes, rimmed red from crying, locked onto Genesis. In that moment, the weight of their shared loss hung heavy between them.

"Justina," Genesis managed, his voice barely above a whisper. "I'm so sorry."

She nodded, unable to speak. Talisa rushed forward to embrace her, Genesis found himself face to face with his grandson. The boy's innocent eyes, so like his father's, gazed up at him curiously.

"Hey there, little man," Genesis said softly, gently ruffling the child's hair. A lump formed in his throat as he thought of all the moments Amir would miss.

"We're gonna take care of you," he promised, more to himself than to the boy. "Both of you. That's a promise." Genesis then turned to Justina's mother. "It's always a pleasure to see you, Chantal." They exchanged a warm embrace. "I'm glad you're here."

"I wouldn't be anyplace else. We loved Amir like a son," Chantal said still in shock that he was gone.

As Justina, Chantal, and Talisa made their way deeper into the room, Lorenzo entered. Genesis immediately noticed him and their eyes met. "I can't believe you actually came!" Genesis exclaimed with joy upon seeing his old friend.

"Man, you my brother. I'll always show up for you," Lorenzo assured him.

"I'm grateful. Did Dior come too?" Genesis inquired.

"Absolutely. She stepped away to use the restroom," Lorenzo replied.

"Great. I look forward to seeing her. Please, take a seat at the table," Genesis said with a smile. "I'll be in there shortly.

"I hope everyone's condolences aren't too overwhelming for you," Supreme remarked when he walked over to the bar and stood next to Genesis.

"I'd be lying if I said it wasn't hard but I'm handling it. I want to thank you for welcoming Lorenzo into your home and including him at this dinner. I know he has a complicated past with Precious, so I am grateful," Genesis nodded in appreciation.

"This isn't about me. We are here because we all care deeply about you and Amir," Supreme acknowledged, emphasizing the importance of their friendship and family unity.

Genesis and Supreme continued to stand near the bar in the corner of the living room, the festive hum of the family gathering providing a faint backdrop. Genesis poured himself a glass of whiskey, his movements deliberate, as Supreme observed him, sensing this moment held more significance than just a simple thank you for welcoming Lorenzo into his home. Supreme had a hunch about what it might entail.

Supreme leaned against the bar. "So, are we going to talk about why Genevieve and Renny didn't show? I know you were looking forward to seeing your sister."

Genesis exhaled heavily, swirling the amber liquid in his glass before taking a slow sip. "They wanted to be here," he said finally, his voice low. "But it wasn't safe."

Supreme's tone and expression showed concern. "Not safe? What do you mean?"

Genesis set the glass down, his jaw tightening. "Renny's been getting heat from some people down south. Old business he didn't clean up the way he should have. I told him to stay put, keep Genevieve out of sight until I can get a handle on it."

Supreme nodded slowly, his expression sympathetic. "You think it's serious?"

"Serious enough for Renny to reach out to me for help," Genesis replied. His voice hardened, his eyes darkening. "I won't risk her getting caught in the crossfire. Not Genevieve. Not with everything else going on."

Supreme tilted his head, studying his friend. "You've got a lot of fires burning, Genesis. You sure you can put this one out too?"

Genesis had a steely scowl, his stubbornness unwavering. "I'll do whatever I have to. Nobody touches my family, Supreme. Nobody."

Supreme nodded, a flicker of understanding and respect passing between them. "Alright. Let me know if you need backup. You know I got you."

Genesis gave him a faint smile, lifting his glass. "I know." They clinked their glasses together in a silent toast, though the weight of Genevieve's absence lingered in the air.

The somber atmosphere was suddenly punctuated by the arrival of a tall, well-dressed man with a carefully cultivated air of concern. Desmond, Justina's ex-husband, strode into the room with patent confidence.

"My deepest condolences," he said, his voice a low rumble as he approached Genesis. "Amir was... a good man."

Genesis nodded stiffly. "Appreciate you coming, Desmond."

As Desmond made his way to Justina, Genesis watched their interaction intently. Justina's body language shifted subtly – a slight stiffening of her spine, a quickening of her breath. Desmond placed a hand on her lower back, the touch lingering a fraction too long to be purely comforting.

"How are you holding up?" Desmond murmured; his lips close to Justina's ear.

She glanced up at him, a mix of guilt and longing flashing across her face. "I'm managing," she whispered back, her fingers brushing against his as she adjusted her hold on her son.

Genesis' eyes narrowed. Something was off about their dynamic, but he couldn't quite put his finger on it.

Across the room, Aaliyah and Angel huddled together, their heads bent in conspiratorial whispers. They surveyed the gathering with sharp, calculating gazes.

"You see how Desmond's hovering around Justina?" Aaliyah muttered. "Something ain't right there."

Angel nodded, keeping her gaze fixed on the two. "I'm surprised Desmond decided to come. I know he's on good terms with Genesis, but he's also Justina's ex-husband. Then again, they were all working together to raise baby Desi, so it makes sense for him to show support for Amir," Angel said with a tinge of doubt.

Aaliyah raised an eyebrow, her intuition always sharp when it came to reading people. "There's more to it, I can feel it. Desmond isn't just here out of the goodness of his heart."

Angel considered Aaliyah's words, a frown marring her usually serene expression. "You think he's got another agenda?"

Aaliyah's glare never left Desmond and Justina as she spoke, her tone dripping with sarcasm. "Whatever it is, I'm sure Justina is a willing participant. I wouldn't be shocked if she ends up back in Desmond's bed," Aaliyah scoffed. "Let's keep our eyes and ears open. There's more to this story than they're letting on."

Meanwhile, as the chatter and mournful tones filled the room, Dior slipped in quietly, her presence adding a breath of fresh air to the heavy atmosphere. Lorenzo's eyes still lit up at the sight of her, a smile spreading across his face.

"Dior, I was beginning to think you got lost on your way to the bathroom," Lorenzo said, reaching out to take her hand in his.

"I mean this place is certainly big enough. I have a feeling this is going to be quite the dinner," Dior replied warmly, squeezing Lorenzo's hand.

As everyone prepared for dinner, a gentle knock at the door drew Precious' attention. Kyra, stepped into the room. Her warm smile contrasted sharply with the somber atmosphere.

"Kyra, you made it," Nico called out, his face lighting up as he moved to greet her.

Precious watched as Nico took Kyra's hand, his touch lasting longer than necessary. The nurse's cheeks flushed slightly as she gazed up at him.

"You've done so much for me, I wanted to be here for you," Kyra said with fondness.

"We've done so much for each other," Nico clarified.

Kyra smiled. "I know this must be hard for

you and everyone else here. You all have been through so much."

Nico's shoulders slumped; the weight of his grief visible. "It's been tough but having you here... it helps."

Precious cleared her throat. "Dinner's about to be served. Shall we?"

The group filed into the dining room, taking their seats. Precious and Supreme believed it was only appropriate Genesis sat at the head of the expansive table. He surveyed the faces of his family and associates. The air crackled with immense sorrow.

Talisa leaned in, "You okay, baby?"

Genesis nodded, squeezing her hand under the table. "Let's just get through this."

Genesis inhaled deeply, centering himself and squaring his shoulders. The night was far from over, with challenges and battles looming ahead, but for now, his priority was clear: his family and the legacy he vowed to preserve.

Chapter Three

Unspoken Truths

Genesis stood at the head of the dining table, his hands gripping the polished mahogany edge. His eyes swept across the room, taking in the faces of his family and friends. Each familiar visage was a stark reminder of Amir's absence, the empty chair at the far end of the table a void that seemed to swallow the warmth from the room.

"Welcome, everyone," Genesis said, his voice steady despite the turmoil within. He forced a smile, feeling it strain against his cheeks. "It's good to have you all here tonight to celebrate my son Amir."

As he spoke, his gaze lingered on the huge, framed photo of Amir that Precious had placed on a gold metal ornate easel stand. The sight of his son's confident grin sent a sharp pang through his chest. Genesis swallowed hard, pushing down the lump in his throat.

How can I stand here and play host when Amir's killer is still out there? The thought gnawed at him, threatening to shatter his carefully constructed facade.

"Please, enjoy the meal," Genesis continued, gesturing to the spread before them. "Amir always loved a good family dinner."

As he took his seat, Genesis felt Talisa's hand come to rest gently on his arm. He turned to meet her concerned gaze, seeing the worry etched in the furrow of her brow and the tightness around her eyes.

"I'm here for you." Talisa whispered, her thumb tracing soothing circles on his skin.

Genesis nodded, covering her hand with his own. "I never doubt that which is one of the many reasons I adore you. But I'm fine," he murmured, even as he felt the storm of grief and anger churning inside him.

Talisa's eyes searched his face, unconvinced. She leaned in closer, her voice barely audible.

"You don't have to pretend with me, Genesis. I know how much you're hurting because I'm hurting too. I was robbed of so much time with our son because of Arnez and now I have been robbed again because of Maverick."

For a moment, hearing what his wife said, Genesis felt his mask slip, the pain raw and visible in his eyes. Then he blinked, rebuilding his walls. "We have to be strong," he said, as much to himself as to Talisa. "For the family."

As conversations began to hum around the table, Genesis felt Talisa's grip on his arm tighten slightly. It was a silent promise of support, a reminder that he wasn't alone in this fight. But even as he drew strength from her presence, Genesis couldn't shake the feeling that this dinner was just the calm before the storm.

Justina shifted uncomfortably in her seat, her young son Desi squirming on her lap. Her eyes darted across the table, meeting Desmond's intense gaze for a fleeting moment before quickly looking away. She hugged Desi closer, as if the innocent child could shield her from the tumultuous emotions threatening to overwhelm her.

Justina's heart raced as she tried to focus on Desi, running her fingers through his tight curls. But her eyes, betraying her inner turmoil, kept drifting back to Desmond. His presence across the table was like a magnetic force she couldn't resist.

"Mommy, I'm thirsty," Desi whined, tugging at her sleeve.

"Okay, baby," Justina whispered, grateful for the distraction. She reached for his sippy cup with a trembling hand. She then grabbed her glass of water taking a long sip to steady herself.

Desmond leaned forward, his voice luring and smooth. "Is there anything you need, Justina?"

The way he said her name sent a shiver down her spine. Justina swallowed hard, torn between the heartache for Amir and the electric current Desmond's words sent through her.

"No, I'm... coping," she replied, her voice barely above a whisper. "It's hard, you know? Amir was..." She trailed off, unable to finish the sentence.

Desmond nodded, his eyes never leaving hers.

"I know. He was family. But you've always been strong. You'll get through this for baby Desi."

Justina felt a pang of guilt at the warmth spreading through her chest at his words. She shouldn't be feeling this way, not here, not now.

But the unspoken connection between them was undeniable.

"How's work been?" Desmond asked, his tone casual but his eyes intense. "Still pulling those long nights?"

Justina tensed, recognizing the loaded question. Those "long nights" had often been their cover, their excuse for stolen moments together. She glanced around nervously, praying no one else picked up on the subtext.

"It's... busy," she managed, her voice strained. "Always busy."

"Work? Justina, you got a job. Please tell me about it," Aaliyah interjected herself into the conversation.

"I've been doing charity work. That's all," Justina explained.

"What kind of charity work?" Aaliyah persisted.

"This is not the time for an interrogation, Aaliyah." Justina tried to shut down the questioning.

"I call bullshit," Aaliyah muttered under her breath, loud enough for only Angel to hear her.

Across the table, Kyra's gaze flitted between Justina and Desmond. Though new to the family dynamics, her keen observational skills picked up on the undercurrent of tension. She noted how Justina's fingers fidgeted with her napkin, her eyes darting nervously around the room.

Kyra sat back, intrigued. Her gaze swept the table, taking in the various alliances and tensions. Genesis and Nico seemed to be having a silent conversation with their eyes, while Supreme kept glancing between them, his expression rigid. Talisa's hand never left Genesis' arm, her touch a constant anchor amidst the swirling undercurrents.

The clink of silverware against china plates punctuated the air as servers glided into the room, bearing trays laden with the first course. Kyra watched as bowls of creamy lobster bisque were placed before each guest, the rich aroma wafting through the air.

"This looks delicious," Kyra commented, trying to break the tension.

Genesis nodded, his smile not quite reaching his eyes. "Amir's favorite," he said affectionately, his voice barely audible over the gentle scraping of spoons against bowls.

Conversation resumed, a veneer of normalcy settling over the group like a thin blanket of snow, fragile and ready to melt at any moment. Kyra observed as everyone fell into the familiar rhythms of a family dinner, the facade so practiced it was almost believable.

"How's work been, Nico?" Talisa asked, her tone light but her eyes sharp.

Nico paused, his spoon halfway to his mouth. "Busy," he replied after a beat. "You know how it is."

Kyra didn't miss the loaded glance that passed between Nico and Genesis. She wondered what lay beneath the surface of that simple exchange.

As she sipped her soup, Kyra found herself drawn into the intricate dance of unspoken words and hidden meanings. It was like watching a complex chess game where every move held significance beyond the obvious. She knew all too well, from her own recent encounters with them that beneath this carefully crafted veneer of normalcy, something dangerous was brewing.

Genesis set down his spoon, his movements measured and deliberate. He reached for his glass, the crystal catching the soft light of the dining room chandelier. As he stood, a hush fell over the table, all eyes drawn to his commanding presence.

"Family," he began, his deep voice steady despite the pain that flashed in his eyes, "I'd like to propose a toast to Amir. To a son, a brother, a friend who was taken from us far too soon."

He raised his glass, the amber liquid within catching the light. "To Amir," Genesis said, his voice cracking slightly on the name.

"To Amir," the room echoed, a chorus of voices united in grief.

As glasses clinked together, a heavy silence descended upon the room. Each person seemed lost in their own thoughts, the weight of Amir's absence pressing down on them all.

Talisa's eyes remained moist as she gazed into her glass, lost in thoughts of the son she had been separated from for so many years. She was reminiscing on the precious moments they shared when they finally reunited after everyone presumed, she was gone forever. Those moments together she would cherish and held close to her heart.

On the other side of the table, Angel and Aaliyah leaned into each other, their shared sorrow palpable. The connection formed between Amir, Aaliyah, and Angel during their abduction would never fade. Their bond was unbreakable.

Genesis remained standing, his eyes sweeping over his family. In the silence, he allowed himself a moment of vulnerability, his shoulders slumping slightly under the excruciating pain of his loss and the responsibility he carried.

As the patriarch of both his family and his empire, Genesis knew the road ahead would be treacherous. But looking at the faces around him, he also knew he wasn't alone in this fight. Nico, Supreme, T-Roc, and Lorenzo all locked eyes with him, a silent pact. They were all prepared to unite and seek revenge for Amir, regardless of the consequences.

Chapter Four

Echoes of the Past

As the moments stretched on, the tension at the table was thick and oppressive, suffocating the room. Genesis knew each person seated was wrestling with their own demons, their own guilt and regrets. He struggled to find the right words to bring them all together, to channel their grief into something productive.

"Amir wouldn't want us to dwell in sorrow," Genesis finally said, his voice cutting through the heavy silence. "He'd want us to stand strong, to keep pushing forward. And that's exactly what we're gonna do."

He looked around the table, making eye contact with each person. "We're family," he continued, his voice gaining strength. "And family sticks together, no matter what. Amir might be gone, but his spirit lives on in each of us. Let's honor him by staying united, by showing the world that we're unbreakable."

As Genesis finished speaking, he could see a shift in the room. The sorrow was still there, but it was now tinged with determination. They were ready to face whatever came next, together.

The silence that followed Genesis' words was suddenly broken by Supreme's deep voice. "We should set up a youth center in Amir's name," he said, his eyes bright with purpose. "Give these kids a place to go, keep 'em off the streets. Give them the opportunities Amir always had growing up and his own son will have. It's what Amir would've wanted."

A ripple of reactions spread across the table. Aaliyah's face lit up, nodding vigorously. "That's perfect!" she exclaimed, her voice rich with emotion. "Amir always wanted to make a difference, and he did in each of our lives."

Nico leaned in; his brow creased as he pondered. "We could use that abandoned warehouse on 7th and turn it into something special." His proposal was filled with optimism and hope.

Genesis felt a surge of pride and determination. This was a chance to reshape their legacy. He gave a subtle nod, his mind already racing with possibilities.

As the main course arrived, steaming plates of herb-crusted lamb and roasted vegetables, the atmosphere in the room continued moving in a positive direction. The earlier heavy silence gave way to a buzz of conversation, still tinged with grief but now animated by purpose.

Talisa, serving herself a portion of vegetables, leaned in close to Genesis. "This could be our chance," she whispered, her eyes shining with hope. "To do something good, something lasting and in our son's name."

Genesis squeezed her hand, his throat tight with sentiment. "You're right, this is the time for a change."

Kyra, observing the interactions around her, felt a spark of inspiration. "I could volunteer to teach art classes," she offered hesitantly, her voice growing stronger as heads turned her way. "It might help some kids express themselves, you know?"

The conversation flowed, ideas bouncing

back and forth. Genesis watched it all, a bitter-sweet ache in his chest. They were navigating their grief together, finding a way forward. But beneath it all, he knew the road ahead would be far from easy. The youth center was just the beginning. There were harder choices to come, choices that would test them all.

As the main course plates were cleared, Genesis caught Nico's eye and gave a subtle nod. They rose almost in unison, excusing themselves under the pretense of refilling drinks.

In the dimly lit kitchen, Genesis leaned close to Nico, his voice barely above a whisper. "I got word from Silvano that Maverick's crew has been moving in on the east side."

Nico's face toughened. "I got eyes on his operation too. Lately he's been sloppy. We might be able to take him out tonight if you give the word."

Genesis felt the familiar rush of adrenaline, the instinct to strike hard and fast. But Amir's face flashed in his mind, and he hesitated. "We do this smart, not bloody. I want him cornered, not martyred."

"You sure about this?" Nico pressed, searching Genesis' face. "This ain't just business anymore. It's personal."

Genesis gripped the edge of the counter, his

knuckles white. "That's exactly why we can't fuck this up. We take him down, but we do it clean. No collateral damage. We will take our time. Maverick's death will be slow and painful."

Nico nodded slowly, understanding the depth of Genesis' words. As they returned to the dining room, Talisa met his eyes as Genesis sat back down, concern etched on her face. She leaned in close, her hand finding his under the table. "Whatever you're planning," she whispered, her breath warm against his ear, "I'm with you. All the way."

Genesis turned to her, struck by the fierce loyalty in her eyes. In that moment, he made a decision that would change everything. "I'm gonna end it, Talisa," he stated, his voice thick with emotion. "All of it. The drugs, the violence, the empire. It's time to build something new."

Talisa's eyes widened in disbelief. She squeezed his hand tightly, wordlessly conveying her support.

Genesis' promising proclamation to his wife seemed to be the perfect transition to everyone indulging in the assortment of decadent desserts being served. A massive tray of tiramisu, individual molten lava cakes, and fresh fruit tarts sat in the center of the table, alongside bowls of home-made vanilla ice cream and delicate chocolate truffles.

Desi giggled as he struggled to balance a spoonful of ice cream, eventually letting it plop back into the bowl with a laugh that echoed across the room. Genevieve leaned over to help him; her own face smeared with a bit of powdered sugar from her fruit tart.

"Looks like someone's got a sweet tooth," Precious said, her lips curving into a warm smile as she glanced at the children.

"I think it's genetics," Talisa quipped, dabbing her napkin at the corner of her mouth. "Genesis said Amir was the same way when he was that age."

The room grew quiet for a moment, the mention of Amir hanging in the air like a soft ache. Genesis, seated at the head of the table, cleared his throat. "He would've loved this spread," he said, his deep voice cutting through the silence.

Supreme nodded, raising his fork in a small gesture. "He loved a good meal. I'll give him that, but don't we all."

The moment passed as laughter and conversation picked up again, the bittersweet memories of Amir woven seamlessly into the celebration. Aaliyah and Angel leaned close to each other, whispering about something as they picked at their desserts, their sharp glances darting occasionally toward Justina. Across the table, Nico poured another glass of champagne for Kyra, who smiled shyly as their hands brushed.

"Alright, I think I've had my fill," Lorenzo said, leaning back in his chair with a satisfied sigh. He glanced at Dior, who dabbed delicately at her lips with her napkin, her eyes crinkling with amusement.

As the plates were cleared and the last bits of dessert were savored, the group began to rise from their seats. Precious, ever the gracious hostess, stood first, her voice cutting through the hum of conversation.

"Let's move this to the parlor room," she said with a smile. "We've got coffee, tea, wine more champagne, and a warm fire waiting for us. Everyone, please make yourselves comfortable."

The guests began to file out of the dining room, their laughter and chatter spilling into the adjoining rooms. Desi tugged at Genesis' hand, pulling him toward the tree, while Talisa and Genevieve followed close behind them.

In the parlor room, the atmosphere grew more relaxed. Conversations sparked in small groups—Nico and Supreme leaned against the bar, deep in discussion, while Kyra joined Dior and Lorenzo on the sofa. Aaliyah and Angel, wine-glasses in hand, huddled in a corner, their voices hushed as they exchanged knowing glances.

Precious stood near the grand fireplace, the flames casting a warm glow on her flawless skin as she sipped her glass of red wine. Her eyes, sharp and calculating, darted across the room to where Lorenzo sat. He was leaning slightly to-ward Dior, his expression loving and affectionate as they talked in hushed tones. The sight made something twist uncomfortably in Precious' chest, though she quickly masked it with a smirk.

She wasn't alone for long.

"Well, isn't this cozy," Chantal's voice purred from behind her, the tone dripping with faux sweetness.

Precious didn't need to turn around to know who it was. She placed her wineglass on the mar-ble mantel and turned slowly, her posture poised and deliberate.

"Chantal," Precious said, her smile tight. "Didn't think you'd make it tonight. It's been... what? A decade since you graced us with your presence. How was the lunatic asylum...I meant insane asylum...hell, let's just call it a mental ward?"

Chantal smiled back. "Oh, after all these years, I'm still in recovery, so I advise you to tread carefully. I kid...I kid," she scoffed sarcastically. "But um, besides the devasting loss of Amir, I've been blessed. And it's not every day I get to celebrate with family. Or... close acquaintances." Her gaze flicked meaningfully toward Lorenzo and Dior.

Precious tilted her head, her perfectly arched brow raising slightly. "Family, huh? You mean Justina, or are you talking about Lorenzo?"

Chantal's laugh was light, but there was an edge to it. "Oh, Lorenzo and I go way back. You know that, Precious. But I think it's cute how he's moved on to... Dior. She seems sweet. Simple, but sweet."

Precious' smile didn't waver, though her eyes darkened. "Funny, I don't remember Dior being part of this conversation. But since you brought her up, you sound a bit jealous. I'll admit—it's refreshing to see Lorenzo with someone who's genuine. Someone who doesn't need to rely on theatrics to get attention. You know, like how you put on that performance at my daughter's murder trial, for the crime you actually committed."

Chantal's lips curved into a sharper smile, her hand resting lightly on her hip. "I put that unfortunate time in my life behind me. However, is that what we're calling Lorenzo's lady love? Genuine? Or just someone who doesn't know him as well as we do?"

There was transparent conflict between the women. An unspoken war fought with calculated words and rehearsed smiles.

"Well," Precious said, picking up her glass again and swirling the wine, "if she doesn't know, I'm sure Lorenzo will fill her in eventually. He always did love to talk about the past... when he wasn't busy creating new memories."

Chantal took a step closer, her tone dropping just enough to be heard only by Precious. "Funny you mention memories. I seem to recall one where you thought Lorenzo was yours. And yet, there he was, at my door."

Precious' smile froze, but she recovered quickly, her voice cutting like glass. "Are you sure that wasn't the other way around. It was his relationship with me that sent you over the edge. It doesn't matter," Precious swung her hand dismissively. "At your door, maybe. But it's not about who had him for a night, Chantal. It's about who he *chose* to build a life with."

The implication was clear, and Chantal's eyes flashed with irritation.

Before either could say more, a burst of laughter drew their attention. Lorenzo leaned toward Dior, his hand resting gently on hers as she laughed at something he said. His stare completely engaging, the kind of look both Precious and Chantal knew all too well.

"Looks like we're both yesterday's news," Precious taunted, relishing in Lorenzo's interaction with Dior and how it affected Chantal.

Chantal let out a light laugh, brushing a strand of hair from her shoulder. "Maybe. But some headlines are worth revisiting," her tone airy but with a hint of venom.

With that, Chantal turned and walked away, leaving Precious standing by the fireplace, her grip on her wineglass tightening. Across the room, Lorenzo and Dior remained in their own little world, oblivious to the storm brewing between the two women who once knew him best.

Chapter Five

Whispers of Vengeance

The night air was sharp as Genesis stepped out onto the balcony. The city lights sprawled out before him, a glittering tapestry that felt distant and unyielding. Inside, the laughter and chatter of family carried on, but Genesis needed a moment away from the forced smiles and heavy conversations.

He tightened his grip on the glass of bourbon in his hand, taking a slow sip. He wanted to numb his emotions as it teetered between anguish and rage, the image of Amir's face haunting him. Amir, whose life had been stolen far too soon, whose absence left an ache so deep it threatened to consume Genesis whole.

The sound of footsteps drew his attention. Genesis turned to find T-Roc emerging from the shadows, a cigarette dangling between his fingers. He exhaled a plume of smoke, his eyes narrowing as he studied Genesis.

"Couldn't sit in there anymore, could you?" T-Roc asked, his voice gravelly but tinged with understanding.

Genesis shook his head, his jaw tight. "Every time I look at that table, all I see is the empty seat Amir should be in."

T-Roc nodded slowly, stepping closer. "That kinda pain? It don't go away. But you already know that." He paused, taking another drag of his cigarette. "What you planning to do about it?"

Genesis turned back to the cityscape; his eyes hard. "Maverick got a debt to pay. A big one. And I plan to collect. Only then will I step away and leave the game behind."

T-Roc smirked, the edges of his lips curling around the cigarette. "I figured as much. You got a plan?"

Genesis took another sip of bourbon, the burn doing little to dull his fury. "Not yet. But

I will. This ain't just about revenge, T-Roc. It's about making sure no one else has to feel what we're feeling tonight."

T-Roc nodded; his expression attentive. "You're talkin' about legacy. You gotta be careful. A move like this? It ain't just about Maverick. You take him down, and you gotta be ready for the ripple effect."

Genesis turned to face him; his eyes sharp. "I know. Not only do I have to annihilate Maverick, but I also have to take down everyone affiliated with him. That's why I need each of you to do your part. You're familiar with the logistics of his operation. I need intel, leverage—anything that can put us ahead of him without risking the people I care about."

T-Roc nodded again, with a solemn expression. "You know I got you. But you better be ready for what comes next. Once you start this, there ain't no goin' back. We loss Amir, we can't lose anyone else.

Genesis stared at T-Roc for a long moment, allowing his words to settle over him. "You're right. I've already lost too much. There's no turning back now. I won't stop until I put a permanent end to Maverick and his entire organization."

Inside the estate, Precious stood by the dining room's large bay window, her gaze following Genesis and T-Roc on the balcony. She didn't need to hear their conversation to know what they were discussing. Revenge was in the air, as palpable as the aroma of the dinner that had been served hours earlier.

"You think he's making the right decision to go after Maverick?" Talisa's voice broke through Precious' thoughts.

Precious turned to find Talisa standing beside her, her expression a mixture of worry and determination. "Yes, I do. But even if he shouldn't, he still will," Precious said knowingly. "Genesis won't let this slide. And honestly, I wouldn't either. Don't you want retribution for Amir?"

Talisa nodded, her lips pressing into a thin line. "I just hope he doesn't let it consume him. I've already lost Amir. I can't lose Genesis too."

Precious reached out, placing a reassuring hand on Talisa's arm. "He's stronger than you think. But you're right to be worried. Vengeance can be... blinding."

Their conversation was interrupted by the sound of muffled voices from the other side of the room. Aaliyah and Angel stood in a quiet corner; their heads bent close as they whispered.

"You see how our father's been acting?" Angel murmured; her tone sharp. "He knows something. I can feel it. Whatever Genesis is plotting, our father is in it knee deep."

Aaliyah glanced around before responding, noticing her mother's eyes were on them. "Yep. No doubt Genesis is planning something brutal and I'm all for it."

Angel crossed her arms. "Me too. I want him to tear Maverick apart, piece by piece. And you know what? I hope we're there to witness it. But I want to make sure nothing happens to our dad in the process. We just got him back."

Aaliyah hesitated, her gaze darting toward the balcony. "I'm with you. Genesis better know what he's doing. If this blows up in his face…"

"It won't," Angel interrupted, her voice firm. "It can't. Not this time."

Later that evening, as the family began to disperse, Genesis found himself back inside, his mind still strategizing when he noticed Nico approaching.

"You got a minute?"

Genesis nodded, following Nico into one of the estate's quieter sitting rooms. Once inside, Nico shut the door behind them.

"I know we spoke earlier about this, but my connect reached back out to me a minute ago. I got word from one of our guys downtown," Nico began, his tone urgent. "Maverick's crew is making moves. They've been buying up properties, setting up new fronts. But here's the kicker—there's a weak link. One of his lieutenants, Carlos, has been complaining about how Maverick's running things. Says he's ready to jump ship."

"You think he'll talk?"

Nico shrugged. "He might. If we make it worth his while."

Genesis leaned back against the wall, a slow, calculated smile spreading across his face. "Alright. Then let's make it worth his while," his voice commanding. "What's the play?"

Every word that came out of Nico's mouth was like gold to Genesis, and he listened with rapt attention. Outside, the noise of people talking faded into the distance as everyone began to settle in for the evening.

Nico stepped closer, pulling out his phone and showing Genesis a map of the city. He pointed to a cluster of properties in the East Side.

"This is where Maverick has been setting up shop," Nico began. "We know he's been using these fronts to move his product. But here's the thing—Carlos, one of his lieutenants, has been vocal about his dissatisfaction. Word is, he's pissed that Maverick's been cutting corners and leaving his own people vulnerable."

Genesis raised an eyebrow, his interest piqued. "You sure Carlos wants out?"

"Not just out," Nico said with a roguish grin. "He wants revenge. He's ready to flip on Maverick, but he's playing it smart. Says he wants guarantees—money, protection, and a seat at the table when the dust settles."

Genesis sat down in the chair, his mind racing. It was a tempting opportunity—a crack in Maverick's armor. But something about it didn't sit right.

"And you trust this guy?" Genesis asked, his tone skeptical.

Nico hesitated. "Trust? Not entirely. But we don't need to trust him to use him. If we can get him talking, he could give us the intel we need to take Maverick down from the inside. Hit him where it hurts the most."

Genesis stared closely at the map, the pieces of his plan beginning to align, forming the faint outline of a strategy. Yet he hesitated, weighing his next move—whether to use Shiffon as his opening play or dismantle Maverick's empire piece by piece, starting with his business and ending with his love life.

"Nico, I hear you," Genesis said, his voice measured. "And I get the appeal of flipping one of Maverick's own. But this isn't just about making a move. It's about making the *right* move."

Nico seemed puzzled. "What are you saying?"

Genesis stood; his hands clasped behind his back as he paced the room. "I'm saying we can't afford to rush this. Maverick has survived this long because he's careful. If we come at him half-cocked, we'll end up with more bodies to bury—and it won't be his."

He turned to face Nico, with a penetrating glare. "I want this done right. No loose ends. No second chances. When we take him out, we take *everyone* with him—his crew, his connections, anyone who's ever stood in our way. I want no man left standing."

Nico fully understood the gravity of Genesis' vision. "Okay. So, what's the move?"

Genesis sighed, running a hand over his face. "The move is patience. We continue to gather intel. We vet Carlos. And we make sure, when the time comes, we've covered every angle. I want Maverick to see us coming and know there's nothing he can do to stop it."

Nico's smirk returned, a glint of respect in his eyes. "Cold. I like it."

Genesis gave a grim sneer, the fire of vengeance burning in his chest. "This ain't about being cold. It's about being smart. I lost my son because of Maverick. I'm not losing anyone else."

Nico clapped him on the shoulder, his voice lighter now. "You got it. I'll start putting feelers out. We'll make sure this time, we don't miss."

As Nico left the room, Genesis sank back into his chair, his mind a whirlwind of thoughts. He clenched his fists, the image of Amir's face flashing in his mind.

"This time," Genesis whispered to himself, his voice steely, "we end it for good."

Chapter Six

Betrayal's Kiss

The house had grown quiet, the earlier hum of endless chatter giving way to the gentle creaks and groans of the palatial estate settling into the night. Justina walked silently down the long corridor; her son Desi cradled against her chest. His tiny body had grown heavy with sleep, his warm breath puffing softly against her neck.

Entering one of the guest bedrooms, she carefully laid him down on the plush bed. The nightlight cast a soft glow, and she tucked the blankets around him, smoothing his curls. For a moment, she lingered, her fingers brushing his cheek. Her heart ached with the weight of every-thing—Amir's death, the uncertainty of the fu-ture, and the guilt she carried like a stone in her chest. She turned to leave, but as she reached the door, a figure loomed in the hallway. Desmond.

"Hey," he said softly, his deep voice resonat-ing in the quiet.

Justina froze, her hand tightening on the doorknob. "What are you doing here?" she whis-pered, glancing nervously back at Desi.

Desmond stepped closer, his presence filling the narrow hallway. "I needed to see you," he said simply. His eyes, dark and intense, locked onto hers, and she felt the familiar pull, that magnetic connection she'd been fighting to ignore.

"Desmond..." Her voice was a warning, but it lacked conviction.

"You don't have to say anything," he mur-mured, stepping closer until the heat of him was undeniable. "I just... I couldn't stand watching you from across the room, wanting to hold you, console you and feel you in my arms."

Tears welled in Justina's eyes, her emo-tions a chaotic swirl of grief, guilt, and longing. "I can't—"

"You don't have to do this alone," Desmond interrupted, his hand brushing her arm. The touch was electric, and Justina's breath hitched. "You deserve to be held. To feel something other than this pain."

Before she could stop herself, she reached for him, her fingers curling around his wrist. The unspoken tension between them ignited, the suppressed feelings rushing to the surface.

The kiss came fast and hard, their mouths colliding with a desperate hunger that bordered on reckless. Desmond pulled her against him, his hands sliding down her back as she melted into his embrace.

"This is wrong," she whispered against his lips, even as her fingers fumbled with the buttons of his shirt.

"I know," he murmured, pressing her against the wall. "But it doesn't feel wrong."

Several moments passed and Angel had gone upstairs searching for Aaliyah. As she approached the guest bedrooms, she heard the faint sounds of muffled whispers and soft laughter. Confused, she moved closer, her steps cautious.

When she reached the slightly ajar door, she froze. Her heart dropped as she caught sight of Justina and Desmond, their bodies intertwined, their movements slow and deliberate as they gave in to their desires.

For a moment, Angel couldn't move. Rage and disbelief coursed through her veins, her hands curling into fists at her sides. Amir hadn't even been buried yet, and here was his widow, in the arms of another man—*Desmond, her ex-husband.*

Angel backed away, her breathing shallow as she turned and hurried back down the hall. She didn't trust herself to confront them in the moment, knowing her fury would explode if she did.

Angel found Aaliyah in the game room, scrolling idly through her phone. She stormed in, her face flushed with anger.

"You're not going to believe what I just saw," Angel hissed, in a stinging tone.

Aaliyah looked up, her brow furrowing. "What happened?"

Angel dropped onto the couch beside her, still trying to calm herself. "Justina. She's upstairs... with Desmond."

Aaliyah's eyes widened, shock giving way to cold fury. "What the hell do you mean 'with Desmond'? Like *with* him?"

Angel nodded, incensed. "I saw them, Aaliyah. Together. In one of the bedrooms. They're going at it like some oversexed teenagers."

Aaliyah sat back, her arms crossing tightly

over her chest. Her face contorted with anger. "That trifling—" She cut herself off, as she struggled to find a word strong enough to express her outrage at the situation. "Amir's not even in the ground yet, and she's already hopping into bed with her ex-husband? Oh, she's done lost her fuckin' mind."

"That's the same thing I said. What are we gonna do?" Angel asked, her voice trembling with barely contained rage.

Aaliyah's expression hardened. "First, we don't say anything tonight. This ain't the time or place to air this bullshit out. But believe me, Angel, Justina's about to learn what happens when you disrespect this family. She never deserved Amir. Just a lowdown cunt like her mother."

The sisters' blood boiled with a poisonous mix of disgust and loathing as they made their pact, vowing to hold onto this unforgivable betrayal. They would bide their time, waiting for the perfect opportunity to expose the truth. And when they did, there would be no forgiveness.

The heat between Justina and Desmond was a fire neither of them could extinguish. In the quiet of the dimly lit bedroom, the world outside ceased to exist. The guilt they carried seemed to dissolve in the intensity of their embrace, leaving only raw passion and longing in its wake.

Desmond kissed her intensely, his hands sliding over her body as if memorizing every curve. Justina arched against him, her breath coming in soft gasps as she let herself surrender completely to the moment. Every touch, every kiss was intoxicating, a connection neither of them had experienced before.

"Justina," Desmond crooned, his voice smooth as he trailed kisses down her neck. "I can't be without you. You never stopped belonging to me."

She cupped his face, pulling him back to look into his eyes. Her own were shimmering with tears, overwhelmed with emotions that she couldn't fully articulate.

"I can't be without you either," she admitted, her voice trembling. "When I'm not with you, I feel like I'm drowning, Desmond. But Amir just..." She trailed off, her words choked by guilt.

Desmond pressed his forehead against hers, his hands resting gently on her hips. "I know. I know it's too soon, but we can't pretend anymore. With what happened to Amir... it made me realize how short life is. We can't hide what we feel for each other."

His words struck a chord deep within her, breaking down the last of her defenses. "I love you," she whispered.

"I love you too. Never stopped and always will," Desmond professed.

Tears rolled down her cheeks, and he kissed them away, his touch reverent. "This isn't some mistake, Justina. This is real. It always has been."

They gave in to the fire again, their bodies moving together with a sense of urgency and desperation as if the moment would be snatched away at any second. It was an unspoken vow between them, a promise to hold onto what they had found despite the storm brewing outside the door.

Later, as they lay entwined in the sheets, Desmond traced lazy circles on Justina's bare shoulder. The silence between them was comforting, but reality began to creep back in.

"What do we do now?" Justina asked softly, her head resting on his chest.

Desmond exhaled, his hand pausing in its movement. "We wait, at least until after the funeral. If we come out with this now..." He didn't need to finish the sentence. The fallout would be catastrophic.

Justina sat up, pulling the sheet around her. "I hate lying. But I don't think anyone will ever understand. They'll just see it as betrayal."

Desmond sat up beside her, brushing a strand of hair from her face. "Let me deal with that when the time comes. We don't have to rush this. For now, let's just focus on us. On Desi. When the time is right, we'll tell everyone. Together."

Justina nodded, leaning into him. "I just don't want to lose you, Desmond. Not after everything."

"You won't," he promised, his arms tightening around her. "I'm not going anywhere."

"I needed to hear that because you're my rock. You and Desi are my everything. But for now, this will be our secret," Justina leaned in to kiss Desmond as they laid in each other's arms.

However, unbeknownst to both of them Angel had caught a glimpse of their display of forbidden passion. They were oblivious to the whispers that would spread before they had a chance to explain. The love they had just declared was already teetering on the edge of discovery, and the aftermath of that betrayal would be a storm neither of them was fully prepared for.

Chapter Seven

Dangerous Liaisons

The evening had grown quieter as the guests settled into smaller groups, the earlier tension dissipating into softer conversations and shared moments. In one corner of the expansive living room, Nico and Kyra sat together, a bottle of champagne chilling in a silver bucket between them. Nico poured Kyra a glass, his movements unhurried and intentional, his gaze lingering on her as she accepted it with a smile.

"To new beginnings," he said, raising his glass.

Kyra tilted her head, studying him before clinking her glass lightly against his. "To new beginnings," she echoed, her voice tinged with apprehension.

They sipped in silence for a moment, the weight of unspoken words hanging between them. It was Nico who finally broke the quiet.

"Crazy to think how this all started," he said, his tone reflective. "You taking care of me when I was laid up, barely able to move."

Kyra smiled, her gaze dropping to her glass. "You weren't the easiest patient," she teased. "Stubborn. Always trying to do more than you should have."

Nico chuckled, "What can I say? Sitting still ain't my thing. But you... you kept me sane, Kyra. Those long nights when I thought I'd never get back on my feet... you were there."

Her smile softened, and she looked up at him, her eyes searching his. "I was just doing my job, Nico."

"No," he said firmly, shaking his head. "It was more than that. You didn't just patch me up— you helped give me the strength to keep pushing when I was at my weakest and most vulnerable. You were more than a nurse, Kyra. You became my friend."

She blushed at his words, but there was a flicker of hesitation in her eyes. She set her glass down, clasping her hands together. "And now?" she asked quietly. "What are we now, Nico?"

Nico leaned forward, resting his forearms on his knees. His dark eyes met hers, unwavering. "I think we both know it's more than friendship now," he said, his tone sincere. "But I also know you're holding back. Talk to me, Kyra. What's on your mind?"

She hesitated, her fingers fidgeting with the stem of her glass. "It's not that I don't feel something for you, Nico. I do. But I've seen enough heartbreak to understand how careful I need to be. And there's one thing I need to know before this... before we go any further."

Nico raised an eyebrow. "What's that?"

Kyra took a deep breath, meeting his gaze head-on. "Precious," she said, the name hanging heavy in the air between them. "I need to know if there's still something there. If you still have feelings for her."

Nico blinked, caught off guard by her directness. He leaned back, running a hand over his jaw as he considered his response. "Precious and I... we'll always have a connection," he admitted, his tone careful. "She's the mother of my daughter, and we've been through a lot together. But that chapter is closed. She's with Supreme now, and she's happy. And I'm happy for her."

Kyra paused trying to gage his sincerity. "I believe you," she said after a moment. "But I need to be sure, Nico. I need to know that if I give you my heart, you're not going to break it."

Nico leaned forward again, his hand reaching out to cover hers. "Kyra, listen to me," he said, his voice steady. "You've been by my side when I was at my lowest. You've seen me at my worst, and you never turned away. I'd be a fool to mess this up. If we decide to move forward, I promise you—I won't hurt you. I won't betray your trust."

Her eyes searched his, looking for any sign of hesitation or deceit. She found none. Slowly, she relaxed, her shoulders loosening as the tension eased from her body.

"Okay," she said softly.

Nico smiled, his hand giving hers a gentle squeeze. "Okay."

They sat in silence for a moment longer, the champagne forgotten as the weight of their conversation settled. Finally, Kyra picked up her glass, a small smile playing at her lips.

"To us," she said, raising her glass.

Nico's grin widened as he lifted his own. "To us."

And as their glasses clinked, the spark of something new and undeniable flared between them, a quiet promise of what might come next.

The soft murmur of laughter and conversation from other parts of the house seemed distant as Kyra and Nico shared a lingering smile. The connection between them felt fragile yet undeniable, as though they were on the precipice of something new.

As they sat in quiet companionship, Nico's hand still resting lightly over Kyra's, the sound of heels clicking against the marble floor pulled them back to reality. They turned simultaneously, their private moment disrupted by the arrival of Precious.

She paused in the doorway, her gaze flickering between them, her perfectly arched brows raising slightly. Her fitted emerald-green dress shimmered faintly under the light, and her posture, as always, exuded confidence and poise.

"Am I interrupting something?" Precious asked, her tone light but laced with curiosity. Her lips curved into a faint smile, though her eyes scanned the scene before her, clearly trying to decipher the dynamic between them.

Kyra's cheeks flushed, and she instinctively pulled her hand away from Nico's, reaching for her glass of champagne as a distraction. Nico, however, leaned back in his chair, a slow grin spreading across his face.

"Not at all," Nico said smoothly, lifting his glass in a casual salute. "Just enjoying a quiet drink with Kyra."

Precious tilted her head, her expression unreadable. "Hmm. It didn't seem like *just* a drink," she said, her gaze landing on Kyra, whose flush deepened.

"It's nothing," Kyra said quickly, forcing a smile. "We were just... talking."

Precious stepped further into the room, her heels clicking softly against the floor. She crossed her arms, leaning slightly against the edge of the sofa as her sharp eyes studied them both.

"Talking about what?" she asked, her tone still light but now edged with something else curiosity, perhaps, or even concern.

Nico chuckled, unfazed. "Life," he said simply. "The past, the future. You know, the usual stuff people talk about over champagne."

Precious' gaze lingered on him for a moment before shifting back to Kyra. "Interesting," she said, her tone delicate but probing. "Well, whatever it is, I hope it's a good conversation. We need some peace and positivity on this Christmas Eve."

"It is all love," Nico said firmly, his tone leaving no room for doubt.

Precious studied him, her eyes narrowing slightly before she gave a small nod. "Good. Nico, you deserve some peace. And Kyra..." She turned to the woman she was not completely sold on but was beginning to warm up to, her expression softening. "You've been a blessing to this family. I can't thank you enough for everything you've done for Nico."

Kyra smiled faintly, her nerves easing slightly. "It's my pleasure, Precious. Really."

There was a beat of silence, heavy with unspoken thoughts. Then Precious straightened, her posture regal.

"Well, I'll leave you two to your drinks," she said smoothly. "Just thought I'd check in."

As she turned to leave, Nico called after her. "Precious."

She paused, glancing back over her shoulder.

"I'm good," he said simply, his eyes meeting hers. "You don't have to worry."

Precious held his gaze for a moment, Nico's words resonating with her. He was her first love, and she would always worry about him, but this was Nico's way of saying it was okay for her to let go. Precious nodded, a small, almost imperceptible smile tugging at her lips. "I'm glad to hear that," she said lovingly before disappearing down the hall.

The room fell quiet again, the tension slowly dissolving. Kyra exhaled, her fingers toying with the rim of her glass.

"Well, that wasn't awkward at all," she giggled, her voice tinged with humor.

Nico laughed, leaning closer to her. "Relax. Precious is just... observant. She's always been like that."

Kyra looked at him. "You think she suspects something?"

"Let her," Nico said with a shrug, his smile turning playful. "Doesn't change anything."

Kyra's lips curved into a reluctant smile. Despite the interruption, she felt a growing sense of ease with Nico—a sense of rightness that she couldn't ignore. Maybe it was finally her time to fall in love.

Chapter Eight

The Noose Tightens

The fluorescent lights of the hospital flickered faintly as Caleb stepped off the elevator, a small, wrapped package tucked under his arm. The sterile smell of antiseptic filled the air, mingling with the faint hum of machines from down the hall. It was Christmas Eve, but the hospital was a far cry from the warmth and cheer he imagined most people were experiencing tonight.

Caleb's steps were slow, deliberate, as he made his way toward Shiffon's room. He paused outside the door, his hand tightening on the small gift he'd brought. He inhaled deeply, pushing down the conflicting emotions swirling inside him.

Genesis' words echoed in his mind: *"Shiffon's carrying Maverick's child. She's gotta go."*

It wasn't a suggestion. It was a death sentence. But here Caleb was, standing outside her room, still grappling with the weight of his loyalty to Genesis and the moral line he felt himself nearing. He knocked softly before pushing the door open. Shiffon looked up from the hospital bed, her face lighting up with a tired but genuine smile.

"Caleb," she said, her voice sweet and warm. She shifted slightly, her hand instinctively resting on her belly. "I can't believe you came to see me, although I'm glad you did."

Caleb stepped inside, the corners of his mouth lifting into a small smile. "It's Christmas Eve, Shiffon. Couldn't leave you here alone, could I?"

Her smile widened, though her face was still dull, her movements slow as she adjusted her position. The shooting had taken a toll on her, but she was recovering. And so, thankfully, was the baby.

"I brought you something," Caleb said, holding out the small package.

Shiffon's eyes danced with excitement, a hint of surprise crossing her face. "You didn't have to do that."

"Maybe not," Caleb said, his voice mellow. "But I wanted to."

She took the gift, unwrapping it carefully to reveal a small, hand-knit baby blanket. Her fingers brushed over the cashmere fabric, and tears welled in her eyes.

"Caleb," she whispered, her voice quivering. "This is... thank you. It's beautiful."

He shrugged, a trace of sheepishness creeping into his expression. "Figured the little one could use something special."

Her hand rested on the blanket for a moment before moving back to her belly. "It means so much. More than you know."

Caleb's jaw tightened as he watched her, the warmth of the moment battling with the cold reality of what Genesis had ordered him to do.

"How are you feeling?" he asked with concern.

"Better," she said with a small nod. "The doctor says the baby's doing well. That's all that matters."

Shiffon always came across as tough and fierce, but this pregnancy brought about an almost childlike sweetness. This innocence she was exuding cut him like a blade. She had no idea the danger she was in, no idea that the man standing before her was torn between protecting her and carrying out her execution.

"Glad to hear," Caleb said, forcing his voice to stay steady. "That's good."

Shiffon's eyes remained fixed on Caleb. "You seem... distracted," she said. "Is everything okay?"

Caleb hesitated, the heaviness of the moment pressing down on him. "It's just... been a rough couple of weeks," he said finally. "Lot on my mind."

"I get that. But even with all you have going on, you've been so kind, Caleb. Coming here, checking on me... it means the world."

He looked away, unable to hold her gaze. He didn't feel like the kind man she thought he was. He felt like a coward, standing there knowing what he knew and not saying a word.

"Shiffon," he began, his voice hesitant.

"Yeah?"

He paused, his fists clenching at his sides. For a moment, he considered telling her everything—about Genesis' plans, about the danger she and her child were in. But he stopped himself. He couldn't.

Instead, he shook his head. "Just... take care of yourself, alright? And the baby."

She smiled sweetly, her eyes glistening. "I will. Thank you, Caleb. For everything."

As Caleb left the room, his expression hardened. The guilt and turmoil churned in his chest, but he couldn't afford to let it show.

He pulled out his phone, his fingers hovering over Genesis' number. He had to try, one last time.

The line rang once before Genesis picked up. "What is it?"

Caleb exhaled. "Boss, we need to talk about Shiffon."

"What's there to talk about?" Genesis replied coldly. "She's carrying Maverick's blood. That's all I need to know."

Caleb swallowed hard. "I get it, but the baby is innocent. Killing Shiffon and her child won't bring Amir back."

There was a long pause on the other end of the line, the tension palpable.

"You think I don't know that?" Genesis said finally, his voice a quiet storm. "But this isn't just about Amir. This is about sending a message. Maverick took my son. He doesn't get to walk away from that without losing everything."

Caleb closed his eyes, his grip tightening on the phone. "I just... I don't wanna do this, Genesis. There's gotta be another way."

Genesis' voice turned ominous. "You do what I tell you to do, Caleb. Or I'll have someone else get it done. Clear?"

Caleb's throat tightened, but he forced himself to respond. "Clear."

The line went dead, and Caleb lowered the phone, his hand shaking slightly. He didn't know how much longer he could walk this tightrope between loyalty and his own conscience.

But one thing was certain: if Genesis didn't change his mind, Shiffon's life—and the life of her unborn child—hung by the thinnest of threads.

Chapter Nine

A Christmas to Remember

The morning sunlight streamed through the massive floor-to-ceiling windows of Precious and Supreme's estate, casting a golden glow over the impeccably decorated living room. The majestic Christmas tree stood tall in the center, adorned with sparkling ornaments and twinkling lights, its base overflowing with gifts each carefully wrapped in shimmering paper, tied with bows and ribbons of all sizes and colors. The smell of freshly brewed coffee, cinnamon rolls, and maple syrup wafted through the air, creating an atmosphere of warmth and joy, even as a cloud of grief lingered among them.

The family gathered in the grand dining room for Christmas breakfast, the long table laden with platters of pancakes, scrambled eggs, smoked salmon, and an assortment of pastries. Despite the laughter and cheerful chatter, Amir's absence was a silent guest at the table, felt by everyone.

Genesis sat at the head of the table; his grandson Desi perched on his lap. The little boy, still in his Christmas pajamas, giggled as Genesis handed him a piece of pancake. His tiny hands eagerly reached for the syrup-covered treat, his innocence a beacon of light in an otherwise heavy-hearted day.

"You're just like your dad, you know that?" Genesis said, his voice thick with emotion. "He used to sit on my lap just like this, making a mess with syrup and pancakes. Couldn't get enough of the stuff."

Desi looked up at him with wide eyes, a sticky smile spreading across his face. "Daddy liked pancakes too?"

Genesis nodded, his throat tightening. "He loved them. Just like you."

Across the table, Justina watched the interaction, her heart aching as she saw the tender-
ness in Genesis' eyes. She wiped a tear away dis-
creetly, her gaze shifting to the empty chair that
should have been Amir's.

"Genesis," Precious said gently, her voice
drawing him back. "Do you want to say something about Amir before we exchange gifts?"

Genesis nodded, his jaw tightening as he
stood, gently placing Desi in Justina's arms. He
looked around the table, meeting the eyes of everyone gathered—Precious, Supreme, Talisa,
Genevieve, Nico, Aaliyah, Angel, Lorenzo, Dior,
Desmond, T-Roc, Chantal and even Kyra, who sat
quietly at Nico's side.

"Family," Genesis began, his deep voice
steady but punctured with pain. "Today is supposed to be about joy, about love, and about being together. But we all know it's not the same
this year. Not without Amir."

A heavy silence fell over the room, the clinking of silverware against plates stopping as everyone turned their full attention to him.

"Amir was more than my son," Genesis continued, his voice cracking slightly. "He was a
brother, a father, a friend. He was the kind of man
who'd give you the shirt off his back, no questions

asked. The kind of man who believed in family above all else."

He paused, his eyes glistening as he looked down at Desi, who stared back at him with a mix of curiosity and innocence.

"Desi," Genesis said softly, crouching to meet the boy's gaze. "Your dad loved you more than anything in this world. He was brave, he was strong, and he was a good man. And I promise you this—every day, I'll make sure you know just how much he loved you. I'll make sure you grow up knowing what a great man he was."

Desi nodded solemnly, his little hand reaching out to touch Genesis' cheek. "I love Daddy," he said simply.

"I know you do," Genesis whispered, pulling him into a tight hug. "And he loved you too."

"Daddy, I love you too," Genevieve smiled up at her father while wrapping her arms around his leg.

The moment was poignant, a shared grief that united everyone in the room. Precious wiped away tears as Supreme placed a comforting hand on her shoulder. Talisa reached out to clasp Genesis' arm; her own emotions barely contained.

After breakfast, the family moved to the living room, where the fireplace crackled warmly, and the Christmas tree shimmered like a beacon of hope. Genevieve and Desi squealed with delight as gift after gift was handed to them—cars, dolls, action figures, books, and even tiny leather jackets, which earned laughter and cheers from everyone.

"This one's from me," Genesis said, handing Desi a small, wrapped package.

Desi tore into it eagerly, revealing a photo album with "For Desi, With Love" engraved on the front.

"What is it?" Desi asked, his little fingers flipping through the pages filled with photos of Amir—laughing, playing, and holding baby Desi.

"It's a book about your daddy," Genesis explained, on the verge of falling apart. "Every picture, every story—so you'll always remember him."

Desi beamed, clutching the album tightly to his chest. "Thank you, Grandpa!"

The room erupted into soft laughter and applause, the heaviness of the day momentarily lifting as Desi's joy became contagious.

As the day wore on, the family exchanged gifts and shared stories of Amir, their collective grief mingling with the warmth of their love for one another. Though the loss was profound, they found solace in the bonds that held them together, determined to honor Amir's memory by continuing to cherish one another.

For Genesis, the day was bittersweet—a reminder of all he had lost, but also a chance to recommit himself to what truly mattered. As he watched Genevieve and Desi play with their new toys, surrounded by the love of family, he felt a flicker of hope.

This wasn't the end. It was a new beginning. One that Amir's legacy would guide them through, no matter what challenges lay ahead.

Genesis sat back in his chair, watching Desi flip through the photo album with innocent delight, pausing to point at each picture and exclaim, "That's Daddy!" with wide-eyed excitement. Across the room, his daughter Genevieve knelt by the tree, carefully unwrapping a dollhouse Supreme and Precious had gifted her. She giggled as she rearranged its tiny furniture, her laughter light and carefree.

The sight filled Genesis with a profound mix of emotions—love, pride, and an aching sense of purpose. Amir's absence was a scar that would never fade, but the face of his daughter and grandson reminded him that the future wasn't lost. It could still be salvaged.

As the chatter and laughter of the family

filled the room, Genesis leaned back, his thoughts shifting to darker territory. His mind accepting what would come next—Amir's funeral preparations. And then Maverick. The man responsible for shattering his world.

Genesis face tightened, his hands curling into fists. The thirst for vengeance consuming his thoughts. Taking Maverick down wasn't just about revenge anymore—it was about ensuring his family's safety. He'd let too many threats grow unchecked, and Amir had paid the price. That wouldn't happen again.

But as the fire of his anger burned, another thought began to take root. For years, Genesis had built his empire on violence and fear. He had justified it as a means to an end—a way to protect his family, to secure their future. But looking into Desi's bright, innocent eyes, he realized that all the power and money in the world meant nothing if it left his family vulnerable, if it perpetuated the same cycle of danger and loss.

He glanced across the room at Talisa, who sat by Genevieve, helping her assemble the dollhouse. Her strength and resilience had always been his anchor, but she had already suffered too much because of his choices. She deserved a life free of fear, as did Genevieve and Desi.

Genesis exhaled slowly. Taking down Maverick would be just the beginning. Once the man who killed his son was gone, Genesis would dismantle the empire he had spent his entire life building. Piece by piece, he would tear it down, replacing it with something real, something legitimate—a legacy his children and grandchildren could be proud of.

Later, as the festivities wound down and the children played with their gifts, Genesis found himself on the balcony overlooking the snow-dusted grounds of the estate. Supreme joined him, a glass of bourbon in his hand.

"You good?" Supreme asked, leaning on the railing beside him.

Genesis nodded, his gaze fixed on the horizon. "I'm getting there," he said.

Supreme studied him for a moment before taking a sip of his drink. "I know that look. You've got something on your mind."

"I've been thinking about the future," he admitted. "About what comes after I deal with Maverick."

Supreme said nothing, waiting for Genesis to continue.

"I've spent my whole life building something I thought would keep my family safe," Genesis said, his voice low. "But all it's done is put targets on their backs. Amir's gone because of me—because of the choices I made. And I can't let that happen again."

Supreme nodded slowly, his expression thoughtful. "You're talking about walking away from it all."

"Not just walking away. Burning it to the ground. Everything—the drugs, the money, the connections—it's got to go. I'll use whatever's left to start over. Build something clean. Something real."

"That's a big move, Genesis. You sure you're ready for the fallout? Walking away from this life... it ain't just about you. It's about everyone who depends on you, everyone who stands to lose when you pull the plug."

"I know," Genesis said firmly. "And I've thought about that. But I can't keep living like this—looking over my shoulder, wondering who's gonna come for my family next. Desi, Genevieve... they deserve better. Talisa deserves better."

Supreme clapped him on the shoulder, "It won't be easy. But if anyone can pull it off, it's you."

Genesis looked at him, a flicker of gratitude in his eyes. "I don't expect it to be easy. But I've made up my mind. After Maverick's gone, I'm done. It's time to build a legacy worth leaving behind."

As the night wore on and the family began to disperse, Genesis knelt by Desi's bed, tucking him in as the boy clutched the photo album tightly.

"Grandpa," Desi murmured sleepily. "Is Daddy happy in heaven?"

Genesis swallowed hard, his throat tightening. He placed a gentle hand on Desi's head, brushing his curls. "Yeah, buddy. He's happy. And he's watching over you every day."

Desi yawned, his eyes fluttering closed. "I love you, Grandpa."

"I love you too, little man," Genesis whispered.

As he stood and turned off the light, Genesis felt a new sense of clarity. The road ahead would be long and filled with challenges, but for his family—for Amir's legacy—he would see it through.

And when the time came, he would step into a new chapter, leaving behind the shadows of his past to create a brighter future for the ones he loved.

The soft hum of conversation and the clinking of glasses filled the living room as the family gathered for the last moments of Christmas Day. Despite the festive decorations and warm fire crackling in the hearth, a quiet heaviness lingered. It was a reminder of what had been lost and what remained unresolved.

Chapter Ten

A Family's Farewell

Genesis stood by the fireplace, staring at the flickering flames. The light danced across his face, highlighting the lines of grief and determination etched deeply into his features. He held a glass of whiskey in his hand, but he hadn't taken a sip. Instead, he turned the tumbler slowly, his thoughts elsewhere.

The family was scattered around the room. Desi sat on the floor, playing with his new action figures, while Genevieve helped him line up his toy cars. Talisa sat on the couch, watching her daughter and grandson with a soft, wistful smile. Across the room, Precious and Supreme were huddled together, quietly discussing plans for the youth center they wanted to build in Amir's name.

Nico and Kyra stood near the Christmas tree; their conversation punctuated by nervous laughter as they danced around the growing connection between them. Aaliyah and Angel whispered in the corner, their sharp glances occasionally darting toward Justina, who sat quietly watching Desi, lost in thought.

It was a moment of peace, fragile and fleeting, as if the family was collectively holding its breath, waiting for the next storm to come. Genesis cleared his throat, drawing everyone's attention. The room fell silent as he stepped forward, his broad shoulders squared, his presence commanding.

"Family," he began, "The last couple days have been about remembering Amir. About celebrating his life and the love he brought into all of ours. But it's also a reminder of what's most important." Genesis paused, his gaze sweeping across the room. "Family. Loyalty. Love. Those are the things that bind us together, that make us stronger. But we've also seen what betrayal can do—how it tears at those bonds, how it leaves scars that never fully heal."

His words seemed to linger in the air, heavy with meaning. Justina shifted uncomfortably, her eyes dropping to her lap. Aaliyah's lips tightened, her hand brushing Angel's arm as if silently urging her to stay quiet—for now.

"But no matter what," Genesis continued, his voice growing stronger, "we have to stick together. We have to protect each other. Because if we don't, we'll fall apart. And that's not what Amir would've wanted. That's not who we are."

There was a moment of silence before Supreme raised his glass. "To Amir," he said, his voice rough with emotion.

"To Amir," the family echoed, their glasses lifting in unison.

Later, as the evening wore on, Genesis stood on the terrace, taking in his last night at Precious and Supreme's palatial estate before heading back to his penthouse in New York City. The cold air biting against his skin as he stared out over the vast, snow-covered grounds. The pool below, usually a shimmering blue oasis in warmer months, was now a reflective sheet of ice, its surface dusted with freshly fallen snow. The gentle sound of the waterfall feature, partially frozen but still trickling, added a faint rhythm to the silence that surrounded him.

He was wrapped in a tailored black coat, the collar turned up against the chill, his hands tucked deep into his pockets. Snowflakes drifted lazily from the overcast sky, catching in his short-cropped hair and settling on the shoulders of his coat. Behind him, the muffled sounds of his family's laughter and conversation seeped through the glass doors, a reminder of the warmth he had temporarily stepped away from.

But Genesis wasn't cold. Not in the way that mattered. The fire in his chest, the searing mix of grief, anger, and determination, burned too hot to be extinguished by something as simple as winter's chill. His dark eyes, usually sharp and commanding, softened slightly as he gazed across the estate's expansive grounds.

He watched the snow blanket the world in pristine white, untouched and clean—a stark contrast to the chaos and blood that had stained his life for decades. The pool, the elaborate Christmas celebration, the estate—they were symbols of the wealth and power they had all built, but today they felt like hollow victories. Amir should've been here.

The thought hit him like a blow, as it always

did when his mind wandered to his son. Amir should have been out there throwing snowballs with Desi, making jokes, and filling the air with his laughter. Instead, the world felt quieter, heavier, as though even nature mourned his absence.

Genesis gripped the cold metal railing, his knuckles whitening. Below, Desi and Genevieve's laughter drifted toward him as they played in the garden, their bright voices cutting through the solemnity of the day. He watched them for a moment, a flicker of a smile crossing his face before the weight of responsibility pulled it away.

He turned his gaze upward, the gray clouds heavy with the promise of more snow. As he stood there, the enormity of his decisions pressed down on him. The vengeance he sought against Maverick felt inevitable, like the falling snow, but it wasn't enough. Once that chapter was closed, there was still the rest of his life—and theirs. Desi, Genevieve, Talisa—they deserved better than the world he had built for them.

Genesis leaned forward, the railing icy beneath his palms, and exhaled deeply. His breath formed a cloud in the frigid air before dissipating, much like the criminal empire he planned to dismantle. It would vanish, piece by piece, and with it, the threats that had already claimed one life too many.

But how do you step away from the only life you've ever known? How do you fight an enemy while preparing to destroy the foundation you've built with your own hands?

Genesis's thoughts were interrupted by the sound of the terrace door sliding open behind him. He didn't turn. He didn't have to. He felt Talisa's presence before she spoke.

"It's cold out here," she said softly, stepping closer and wrapping her arms around herself against the chill.

"It's quiet," he replied, his voice grave. "Needed a minute to think."

Talisa joined him at the railing, her eyes following his to the snow-covered grounds below. "You always think too much when you come out here. What's on your mind?"

Genesis let out a quiet laugh, his breath fogging in the air. "Everything. Amir. Desi. Genevieve. What comes next."

Talisa leaned into him, her warmth seeping through the layers of his coat. "Whatever comes next, we'll handle it. Together."

Genesis nodded; his gaze still fixed on the horizon. "It's not just about handling it, Talisa.

It's about changing it. For good. I can't leave them this legacy of blood and violence. I won't."

Her hand found his, and he turned to look at her, the determination in his eyes mirrored by the unwavering support in hers.

"You don't have to do it alone," she said. "You have me. You have all of us."

Genesis gave her hand a gentle squeeze, his jaw tightening as he looked back out at the snowy landscape. "It's gonna take time. But I'll do it. For them. For us."

The snow fell steadily, blanketing the terrace and pool below, as if offering a clean slate. Genesis stood there, unyielding, knowing that the path forward would be treacherous. But for the first time in years, he felt the faint stirrings of hope.

Talisa, wrapped her arms around Genesis' waist, wanting her husband to feel her endless love.

"You've been amazing through all of this. I have never been prouder of you," she said softly, resting her head against his chest.

Genesis exhaled, his arm coming around her. "It's not enough," he said. "It'll never be enough. But I will make you proud."

Talisa pulled back slightly, looking up at him.

"You're doing what you can, Genesis. That's all anyone can ask and I'm already proud of you."

He exhaled as if freeing a heavy load. "After Maverick, everything changes. I'm ending this life, Talisa. For good. For Desi, for Genevieve—for all of us."

"I believe you," she said, her voice filled with quiet conviction. Talisa began to wonder if her husband was trying to convince himself.

Inside, Precious caught Aaliyah and Angel immersed in conversation. "What's going on with you two?" she asked, her tone light but probing.

Aaliyah crossed her arms, her piercing eyes locking onto her mother's. "You really want to know?"

"Yes," Precious said, now determined to find out what was going on. "Speak."

Aaliyah caught Angel's nod, so she leaned in, lowering her voice. "Justina and Desmond. Angel saw them... together."

Precious' eyes widened slightly, letting what was said sink in. "Are you sure?"

Angel confirmed, her head bobbing up and down. "I saw it happen with my own two eyes. They didn't even wait for Amir's burial," she sighed in disbelief. Angel had developed a strong bond with Amir during their captivity. She was convinced that he had saved her life by taking the brutal beating meant for her. Her loyalty to him, even in death, remained unwavering.

Precious glared at Justina, sending a wave of anger in her direction. "Genesis can't find out about this. Not now. Not yet."

"Then I better keep my distance because I swear, I'm ready to smack the shit outta her. If you all excuse me for a moment, I need a glass of champagne," Aaliyah said storming off.

Aaliyah stepped into the sitting room, the muted glow of the lamp casting soft shadows across the walls. The sounds of **Brandy's Christmas Party For Two** played in the background:

> *To feel your kisses on my skin*
> *Underneath this mistletoe*
> *I know that I can't let you go forever, baby*
> *Can we start again? The season for pleasin'*
> *I know that I need you*
> *I'm down on my knees*
> *Got a little fireplace to keep you warm*
> *The two of us fall back in love this Christmas...*

In her hand, a half-full glass of champagne sparkled under the dim light. She took a slow sip, savoring the effervescence as she let herself breathe in the stillness of the moment and the music soothing her soul. Her mind, however, was anything but quiet.

The image of Justina and Desmond flashed in her thoughts like a jagged shard of glass, cutting into her composure. She gripped the stem of her glass so hard she feared it might snap.

How could she?

The audacity of Justina—Amir's widow, sitting under her parents' roof, sleeping with Desmond, and acting as though nothing had happened—filled Aaliyah with a simmering rage. It wasn't just about Amir's memory, though that alone was enough to make her stomach churn. It was about loyalty, respect, and the utter betrayal of everything Amir had stood for.

Aaliyah tilted her head back, exhaling sharply as she tried to rein in her emotions. She glanced at the glass in her hand, the bubbles swirling up in delicate streams, a stark contrast to the turmoil roiling inside her. Her thoughts drifted, unbidden, to Amir.

Growing up, Amir had been her rock—her confidant, her partner-in-crime, her best friend. They'd shared countless laughs, adventures, and secrets. He'd been the one person who could always make her smile, even on her darkest days. She remembered how he would playfully tease her, his grin mischievous and full of life, and how they'd spend hours talking about their dreams for the future.

But then, one summer, everything had shifted. Their friendship had deepened into something more—a spark igniting between them that neither of them had been able to deny. She smiled faintly, remembering the stolen kisses, the whispered promises, and the way he'd look at her like she was the only person in the world.

They'd tried to keep it casual at first, not wanting to risk their bond. But it hadn't worked. They were magnetic, drawn to each other in a way that was impossible to ignore.

"What if..." Aaliyah murmured, her voice barely audible as she stared into her champagne glass.

What if they had stayed together? What if she hadn't let her selfish, immature ways pull them apart? What if they had gotten married, had a child, built a life together? Would Amir still be alive? Would Desi be *their* son instead of Justina's?

The thought was bittersweet, a combination of longing and guilt. She didn't resent Justina for being the one Amir had chosen—though she initially struggled to accept it, Aaliyah finally made her peace with that. But the fact that Justina was so quick to dishonor Amir's memory by turning to Desmond... that was something Aaliyah couldn't forgive.

Amir deserved better; she thought fiercely.

Aaliyah leaned against the window frame, her gaze drifting to the snowy landscape outside. She could almost picture Amir standing out there, bundled up in a heavy coat, tossing snowballs at Desi while laughing that big, infectious laugh of his.

Her heart ached at the memory. She raised her glass, her voice a quiet whisper. "To you, Amir. You were the best of us."

As she sipped the champagne, she felt the tears prick at the corners of her eyes but refused to let them fall. Amir wouldn't want her to cry. He'd want her to live, to fight, to protect their family. And she would.

Aaliyah straightened, setting her empty glass on a nearby table. Justina's betrayal burned in her mind, but she wouldn't let it distract her from what truly mattered—keeping Amir's legacy alive and holding this family together.

She stepped back into the hallway, her head held high, her resolve stronger than ever.

As the night drew to a close, Genesis returned to the living room, finding Desi curled up asleep on the couch, the photo album still clutched in his tiny hands. He knelt beside him, brushing a hand gently over the boy's curls. "I'll protect you," he whispered. "I'll protect all of you."

But even as he made the promise, a shadow of doubt loomed in the back of his mind. He had enemies, both seen and unseen. And while he was determined to dismantle his empire, he knew that walking away wouldn't be simple. There would be those who would fight to take what he was giving up.

Genesis stood and looked around the quiet room, a sense of foreboding settled over him. The battles ahead would test every bond, every promise, every ounce of loyalty this family had left. But for now, they had each other. And that would have to be enough.

In a dimly lit warehouse on the East Side, Maverick sat at a large metal table, his fingers tapping rhythmically against its surface. Beside him, a phone buzzed with an incoming message. He glanced at the screen, his lips curling into a cold, predatory smile.

"Genesis wants a war," Maverick muttered to himself consumed with the whereabouts of Shiffon and their unborn child. "I'll give him one." He turned to Carlos, his lieutenant, who stood silently nearby. "Time to move. Let's show him what happens when you take from me."

The storm was coming. Genesis would have to weather it together with his family—or they would be torn apart.

A KING PRODUCTION

A Titillating Tale

Mastermind...

A Novelette

JOY DEJA KING

Chapter One

"Mr. Richardson, please come with me," the doctor said, gesturing for Cartier to follow him and a nurse into a room at the hospital.

"How is my wife? Is she getting better?" Cartier asked, concern in his voice as the nurse shut the door behind them.

"I'm afraid I have some unfortunate news to share. Despite our best efforts, Lila has passed away," the doctor informed Cartier somberly.

"I'm sorry doctor, why are we here... where

is my wife?" Cartier demanded, in denial, refusing to believe a word the doctor said.

"Sir, my name is Cynthia Johnson," the nurse spoke up, introducing herself formally. "I've been treating your wife during her recent visits. I can take you to see her, but Lila is no longer with us," she said gently, placing a comforting hand on Cartier's shoulder. "We know this isn't easy, and we're here to support you in any way we can."

"I'm sorry, Mr. Richardson, but I have another patient I need to attend to," the doctor explained. "But if you need anything, Cynthia is available to assist you," he added before leaving.

Cynthia sat down next to Cartier and asked, "Is there anything I can get for you? Would you like to see your wife?"

"I don't want to see Lila like that. I want to remember my wife for the beautiful, vibrant woman that she was. Not..." his voice cracked and trailed off.

"I completely understand," Cynthia said sympathetically. "But I do need you to sign some papers so we can release her personal belongings to you." She handed him a pen and the documents from a manilla envelope.

As Cartier signed the papers, he felt the weight of reality sink in. He remained sitting in the empty room, his face buried in his hands. Cynthia tried to offer comfort, but there was nothing she could do to ease his pain. As a nurse, she had delivered news of loved ones' deaths many times before, but it never got any easier. She always took a deep breath before entering a room, knowing that what she was about to say would change someone's life forever.

Cartier looked up with a distant gaze in his eyes. "What am I going to do without my wife? She's the love of my life." He paused and then corrected himself. "She was the love of my life." He swallowed hard, finally accepting that Lila was no longer with him.

Six Months Later...

"Cartier, our clients will be here in fifteen minutes. Do you want to have the meeting in your office or the conference room?" Callie, his Senior Marketing Executive, asked.

"Let's use the conference room. Please make sure Audra has everything set up and ready. I don't want any delays," he said while reading through some key points he wanted to address during the meeting.

"Actually, Audra is currently training a temp that was sent over to cover for Rachel."

"The receptionist... What happened to her?"

"No idea. Audra mentioned that Rachel called early this morning, saying there was a family emergency, and she needed a few weeks off. Audra's busy with the temp, so I'll have Donovan double check to ensure everything is prepared."

"Just get it done," Cartier said dismissively without looking up from his work. "And close my door."

Callie let out a frustrated sigh as she left Cartier's office. "Audra, can you please wrap up this training and meet me in the conference room? I have more important tasks for you to do." She snapped.

"Of course, Callie. Just give me one moment." Audra gave a polite smile before rolling her eyes once Callie was out of sight. "That woman is so annoying. Just because she's fuckin' the boss, she thinks she's the queen bee."

"Wow, I wasn't expecting that tea to be spilled," Serenity chimed in as she settled into her seat at the receptionist desk. "Especially since I'm only here through a temporary employment agency, so technically I don't even work here."

"That's true, which makes it even easier for me to freely run my mouth," Audra laughed. "Sorry not sorry, but Callie is truly a piece of work. The moment Mr. Richardson's wife died she pounced on him like a dog in heat. And mind you, he was screwing two other women who worked here. Both of them ended up getting fired because Callie thought eliminating the competition would increase her chances of becoming the next Cartier Richardson."

"How long ago did his wife pass away?"

"Lila passed away about six months ago. She was so young; it was unexpected and heartbreaking."

"And he's already involved with three different women?" Serenity asked in shock.

"Yes, and three is all that worked in this office. Mr. Richardson has quite the reputation as a ladies' man. Some say his behavior escalated after his wife passed away as a way to cope with his grief. Others claim he always had multiple women in rotation but was more discreet when his wife was alive."

"Interesting. Well, I'm just here to do my job and stay out of any drama," Serenity replied, eager to start working. "I need the paycheck, not the gossip."

"Girl, I feel you, but I need the paycheck. drama and the gossip," Audra laughed. "Working here is like being in a real-life soap opera, and I love it," she grinned before noticing her boss and his right-hand man walking towards them. "Good morning, Mr. Richardson and Mr. Upton!"

Both men responded dryly with a simple "good morning."

"Do you know where Callie is?" asked Cartier, looking slightly vexed.

"Yes, she's in the conference room," Audra replied, her smile never faltering as she maintained her professional demeanor.

"Thank you," said Cartier, hurrying off in the direction of the conference room.

"If you're not in the know, that's our CEO, Cartier Richardson. And the distinguished gentleman walking with him is Bradley Upton, a key player in our company's success. Some say he's really the brains and moral center behind it all, but his loyalty to Cartier never wavers," explained Audra to Serenity.

Serenity found herself completely focused on Bradley Upton. She was curious about his connection to Cartier for various reasons but kept her thoughts to herself in front of Audra. Instead, she directed her comments towards Cartier specifically.

"Mr. Richardson certainly looks the part. That suit he's wearing must have cost a grip," Serenity observed, taking note of the flawlessly tailored Kiton two-piece suit in tonal plaid, with its sharp notched lapels and white-stitched cotton pocket square. The overall look was effortlessly stylish, thanks to a casual navy Kiton cashmere-blend crew-neck t-shirt worn underneath. Dripping with a few brilliant cut diamonds, Cartier definitely knew how to flaunt his wealth.

"Oh yeah," Audra agreed. "Mr. Richardson plays no games when it comes to fashion. He only wants the best." She paused, realizing they needed to finish their conversation later. "But I better get going to the conference room before I get in trouble for gossiping too much. I'll check in on you later though. You have my cell number if you need anything," she said with a wink before rushing off.

As Serenity tried to process everything, she had learned that morning about Cartier Richardson and Bradley Upton, her phone began ringing non-stop.

"Looks like it's going to be a busy day," she said, feeling a mix of nervousness and excitement about what awaited her at her new job.

P.O. Box 912
Collierville, TN 38027
❀❀❀❀❀❀❀❀❀❀❀❀❀

A KING PRODUCTION

www.joydejaking.com
www.twitter.com/joydejaking
❀❀❀❀❀❀❀❀❀❀❀❀❀

ORDER FORM

Name:

Address:

City/State:

Zip:

QUANTITY	TITLES	PRICE	TOTAL
	Bitch	$17.99	
	Bitch Reloaded	$17.99	
	The Bitch Is Back	$17.99	
	Queen Bitch	$17.99	
	Last Bitch Standing	$17.99	
	Superstar	$17.99	
	Ride Wit' Me	$17.99	
	Ride Wit' Me Part 2	$17.99	
	Stackin' Paper	$17.99	
	Trife Life To Lavish	$17.99	
	Trife Life To Lavish II	$17.99	
	Stackin' Paper II	$17.99	
	Rich or Famous	$17.99	
	Rich or Famous Part 2	$17.99	
	Rich or Famous Part 3	$17.99	
	Bitch A New Beginning	$17.99	
	Mafia Princess Part 1	$17.99	
	Mafia Princess Part 2	$17.99	
	Mafia Princess Part 3	$17.99	
	Mafia Princess Part 4	$17.99	
	Mafia Princess Part 5	$17.99	
	Boss Bitch	$17.99	
	Baller Bitches Vol. 1	$17.99	
	Baller Bitches Vol. 2	$17.99	
	Baller Bitches Vol. 3	$17.99	
	Bad Bitch	$17.99	
	Still The Baddest Bitch	$17.99	
	Power	$17.99	
	Power Part 2	$17.99	
	Drake	$17.99	
	Drake Part 2	$17.99	
	Female Hustler	$17.99	
	Female Hustler Part 2	$17.99	

QUANTITY	TITLES	PRICE	TOTAL
	Female Hustler Part 3	$17.99	
	Female Hustler Part 4	$17.99	
	Female Hustler Part 5	$17.99	
	Female Hustler Part 6	$17.99	
	Princess Fever "Birthday Bash"	$6.00	
	Nico Carter The Men Of The Bitch Series	$17.99	
	Bitch The Beginning Of The End	$17.99	
	Supreme...Men Of The Bitch Series	$17.99	
	Bitch The Final Chapter	$17.99	
	Stackin' Paper III	$17.99	
	Men Of The Bitch Series And The Women Who Love Them	$17.99	
	Coke Like The 80s	$17.99	
	Baller Bitches The Reunion Vol. 4	$17.99	
	Stackin' Paper IV	$17.99	
	The Legacy	$17.99	
	Lovin' Thy Enemy	$17.99	
	Stackin' Paper V	$17.99	
	The Legacy Part 2	$17.99	
	Assassins - Episode 1	$12.99	
	Assassins - Episode 2	$12.99	
	Assassins - Episode 3	$12.99	
	Bitch Chronicles	$40.00	
	So Hood So Rich	$17.99	
	Stackin' Paper VI	$17.99	
	Female Hustler Part 7	$17.99	
	Toxic...	$12.99	
	Stackin' Paper VII	$17.99	
	Sugar Babies...	$12.99	
	Deadly Divorce...	$12.99	
	The Legacy Part 3	$17.99	
	BITCH The Story of Precious Cummings	$17.99	
	Mastermind	$12.99	
	Stackin' Paper VIII	$17.99	
	Stackin' Paper Holiday	$12.99	

Shipping/Handling (Via Priority Mail) $9.85 1-3 Books, $18.40 4-10 Books. For 11 or more $24.75.
Total: $_____FORMS OF ACCEPTED PAYMENTS: Certified or government issued checks and
money Orders, all mail in orders take 5-7 Business days to be delivered